Adapted by Tracey West

Based on the film written by Robert Horn

Disney PRESS

Los Angeles • New York

Printed in the United States of America
First Edition, June 2015
1 3 5 7 9 10 8 6 4 2
V475-2873-0-15107

Library of Congress Control Number: 2014952181
ISBN 978-1-4847-1077-7

For more Disney Press fun, visit www.disneybooks.com
Visit DisneyChannel.com

SUSTAINABLE
FORESTRY
INITIATIVE

Certified Chain of Custody
Promoting Sustainable Forestry

www.sfiprogram.org
SFI-01054

The SFI label applies to the text stock

Chapter 1

"Are we there yet?" Mack asked.

The late summer sun was just setting, glinting off Brady's blond hair as he led Mack down the sandy path. Blindfolded, Mack held tightly to Brady's hand.

"We're not doing that 'blindfold surfing' thing again, are we?" Mack asked. "'Cause that didn't exactly end up being one of your better ideas."

"First of all, that buoy had no business being there," Brady said. "Second, no. We're not going to surf. At least not yet."

The path opened into a clearing. Brady gazed around, proud of his work. Two tiki torches burned brightly. He had hung a sheet between two trees and set up a laptop and two big speakers. Then he'd decorated two beach chairs with flowers and placed them in front of his outdoor movie screen. Behind the screen, ocean waves lapped the shore of a secluded cove. Mangrove trees, their thick, gnarled roots reaching into the water, shaded everything.

It's perfect, Brady thought. *Almost as perfect as Mack.*

Even with her blindfold on, she looked beautiful. Her long brown hair hung in waves that reminded him of the ocean they both loved so much. Her skin had a sun-kissed glow from a summer of surfing. A silver necklace with a flower charm hung around her neck.

Brady stopped inside the clearing.

"Okay, guess where we are," he said.

"Hmmm," said Mack. "I hear waves."

Then she sniffed. "There's salt in the air. Mangrove trees. It's so familiar. . . ."

"You recognize it?" Brady asked hopefully.

"Nope," Mack replied.

Brady was bummed. "Oh."

Then Mack smiled coyly. "Unless it's the clearing between the two twisted palms, next to Wipeout Rock, which happens to be the exact spot where we met three months ago to the day."

Grinning, Brady pulled off Mack's blindfold.

"To the minute, actually," Brady pointed out. "At the beginning of what's turned out to be the most bodacious summer of my life."

"Even the little part where we got trapped in a 1960s beach movie?" Mack asked.

"Even that part," Brady said.

Mack wasn't kidding. Just a few days before, Mack had been paddling into the ocean on her grandfather's surfboard when a storm kicked up. Brady rode out on his Jet Ski to help her. A huge wave wiped them out, and when the water calmed down, they found themselves inside the movie *Wet Side Story*. It had been weird, but totally real.

"I thought for a 'meet-iversary' we could reenact the actual moment we met," he said, walking over to a palm tree. "I was here, watching said 1960s beach movie on my tablet."

"And I thought, 'Who's the surf bum with the ridiculous hair?'" Mack continued. "But then you said . . ."

"'Hey, you want to watch the awesomest movie ever made?' And you said . . ." Brady waited for Mack to chime in. "Come on, say it."

Mack smiled. "I said, 'I don't think "awesomest" is a real word. And even if it is, this movie's hardly it.'"

"And then I said, 'Check it out with me, and if you don't totally dig it, I'll buy you a smoothie,'" Brady continued. "'You win either way.' And . . ."

"We watched the end of *Wet Side Story* together,

and I kind of dug it," Mack admitted.

Brady took a remote from his pocket and hit it. The movie started playing on-screen. Peppy beach music blared through the speakers, and kids in colorful bathing suits sang and danced in the sand.

"Watching it on a tablet just didn't seem festive enough," Brady said.

Mack took it all in: the screen, the torches, the chairs.

It's perfect, she thought. *Almost as perfect as Brady.* Now she thought his tousled blond hair was adorable, and his blue eyes reminded her of the ocean they both loved so much.

"You did all this for me?" she asked.

Brady nodded toward the ocean. "I'd swim to China for you. Or Hawaii. Or whatever's that way. I have no idea what's that way."

Mack grabbed his hand. "You're—"

"The best boyfriend in history?" Brady asked.

"A total cheese ball," Mack said.

Brady smiled. "That, too."

They settled into the chairs to watch the movie. The characters in the film had become real to them after their adventure—real friends. It was strange seeing them on the screen.

The movie played out exactly as Mack and Brady had remembered. The surfers and the bikers argued over who would control Big Mama's, their favorite hangout. Then biker girl Lela and surfer boy Tanner fell in love, and things got tense—until the two groups banded together to stop some bad guys from using their weather machine to drive the surfers and bikers away from the beach.

At the end of the movie, the bikers and surfers gathered together on the beach. Butchy, the leader of the bikers, stepped forward.

"Tanner, we's did it," he said, with a tough-guy accent. "We defeated the villainous lighthouse villains and saved the beach. Who woulda thunk it?"

"I would have thunk it, Butchy," replied super-tan surfer boy Tanner. "I never doubted me for a second."

He smiled, and *ping!* His brilliant-white front teeth gleamed. Then he grabbed raven-haired biker beauty Lela and she smiled up at him.

"Here's what I says," Butchy went on. "I says we all go to Big Mama's together. You know, like in a group."

"I've got a better idea," Tanner said.

"You do?" Butchy asked.

"Of course I do," Tanner replied. "I'm Tanner." Then the music swelled, and the bikers and surfers spread out on the sand and sang the movie's closing song: "Best Summer Ever."

Brady was standing on his seat, singing and dancing along with the movie. When the song finished, he looked at Mack.

"And of course, when the movie ended . . ."

"We went surfing," Mack finished, smiling, as Brady revealed two boards hidden behind a palm tree.

They paddled out on the water and rode the waves under the moonlight. Once they were in deeper water, they sat on their boards, staring at the horizon.

"It's too bad that summers in real life have to end," Mack said with a sigh.

"Hey, it's not over yet," Brady said. "We can light a bonfire, rock some s'mores . . ."

"Brady, tomorrow's the first day of school," Mack reminded him. "I gotta finish the summer reading, print fliers for the new oceanography club, get all my supplies together . . ."

"Right. I gotta do all that stuff, too," Brady said. Then he paused. "Actually, I don't. If I remember to put on my board shorts in the morning, I'm pretty stoked with myself."

Brady was joking, but deep down, something was bothering him.

"Mack, are you nervous about tomorrow? That maybe things'll be different for us at school?" he asked.

"We were in school all last year together," Mack reminded him.

"And we never even met," Brady said. "That's my point. We've only known each other in summer. School's a totally new deal."

Mack thought about it.

"Brady. It's us. We're gonna be fine," she said.

Brady smiled, relieved. "Of course. You're right. It's us."

They looked into each other's eyes.

What an amazing summer, Mack thought. *We've been through so much crazy stuff together. School will be easy!*

Absently, she reached to touch her necklace— but she couldn't feel it!

"Oh, no! No, no, no!" she wailed.

"What's wrong?" Brady asked. "Leg cramp? Jellyfish? Tidal wave?"

"My necklace!" Mack cried. "The one that Lela gave me . . . it's gone. It must have fallen off in the waves." She felt like crying.

"Oh, man, I'm so sorry," Brady said. "You want me to dive for it? Maybe it's still nearby."

Mack shook her head. "No, that would be . . ."

"Like trying to find a tiny necklace in a huge ocean. At night," Brady finished.

Mack stared at the water. A chill washed over her, and she shivered. "Nothing we can do now," she said. "Let's ride one in."

They paddled off.

Beneath them, drifting below the waves, the necklace glowed with an eerie magic. . . .

Chapter 2

The first school bell of the day rang as crowds of kids made their way to Windy Bluff High School, excited to be going back. The school was so close to the beach that you could hear the roar of the waves inside every classroom.

Brady biked up to the school in his usual outfit—a T-shirt, board shorts, and flip-flops. He stopped at a bike rack next to another surfer dressed almost exactly like him—his best friend, Devon.

"Dude-man!" Brady greeted him.

"Bro-hams!" Devon hollered.

They hugged and then launched into a surfer handshake that involved a lot of palm slapping and finger wiggling.

"Welcome back! How was Indonesia?" Brady asked.

Devon's eyes gleamed. "Oh, man. The swells were nectar. Primo pearls, my hombre. The waves were all like, 'Buuma!' And I'd be all like, 'Braa!' I was a one-man stoke machine all summer long."

Brady nodded. "Mondo."

"Beyond mondo, bro," Devon said. "How was your summer? You spend some quality time carving up the tubes?"

"I met a girl," Brady replied.

"No way! You trapped a honey?" Devon asked. "Is she a super-chill surf chick?"

"Well . . . she surfs," Brady replied. Mack was definitely not "super chill."

"So she's one of us," Devon said. "Laid back."

"She . . . lays back, on occasion," Brady said,

thinking about how busy Mack always was. "When she sleeps. Probably."

Devon slapped him on the back. "Excellent! Dude, I can't wait to meet your beach bunny."

Brady cringed inside. Mack did not like to hear a girl called a beach bunny. Or a honey. Or a chick.

"Yeah, just maybe don't call her that, exactly. . . ."

While Brady and Devon headed into the school, Mack had been inside for an hour already, handing out fliers for the Oceanography Club.

"Amy! Welcome back!" she cried, handing a flier to a passing girl. "Save the Beach dance this weekend. Buy a ticket, save a seal! Come on. Who doesn't like seals? Well, sharks, maybe. But they don't like anybody."

A boy walked by, and Mack thrust a flier into his hands. "Russel! Love the pants. Is that hemp? Very eco-conscious. The Oceanography Club's throwing a dance. I know I can count on you to save the planet . . . no pressure."

Then she turned. "Tessa! We've got calc together. Mr. Bosco's supposed to be awesome. And we're throwing a dance."

Tessa looked at the flier. "It's in the gym? Like in PE class?" she asked with a frown.

"Yeah, but there'll be a deejay and free punch. And a crazy smoke-making thingy," Mack said, trying to make the dance sound cool.

As Tessa walked away, a girl ran up to Mack and hugged her.

"Alyssa!" Mack cried, excited to see her best friend.

"Mack!" Alyssa cried.

"How was your summer?" Mack asked.

"Oh, beyond," Alyssa replied. "Science camp was epic. The college tour was fab. And don't even get me started on the student government conference." Then she smiled. "I'm so glad you decided to come back this year."

"Me too," Mack said. It was the best decision she'd ever made. Her aunt had wanted her to go to some fancy prep school, far away from the ocean. But Mack had bravely stood up to her and asked to finish high school at Windy Bluff.

She handed a flier to Alyssa.

"What's this?" Alyssa asked.

"I made a deal with myself," Mack replied. "If I'm staying here, I'm doing things that are important to me. So I'm starting an ocean-ography club—which is pretty convenient, since our school's literally *on* the ocean."

"Supercool. Sign me up," Alyssa said. "Oh, and I've got news. Guess who I hung out with at the student government conference? Spencer Watkins. The literally cutest guy in school. And guess who he thinks the literally cutest girl in school is?" Alyssa elbowed Mack, who just blushed.

"Mack!"

Brady walked up with Devon and gave Mack a hug. She looked down at his feet.

"You're wearing flip-flops. To school," she said, her voice flat.

"I totally am," Brady said proudly. "These are my fancy ones. Mack, this is my boy Devon. Devon, this is my girlfriend, Mack."

Devon and Alyssa looked equally shocked.

"This is your girlfriend?" Devon asked.

"This is your boyfriend?" Alyssa asked at the same time.

"You seem surprised," Brady and Mack said together.

"Oh, no, bro," Devon told Brady. "It's just, you know, she has an actual backpack . . . that looks very full of books."

"And he doesn't seem to have a bag at all," Alyssa told Mack.

"I do not have a bag. I do, however, have a pen," Brady said, reaching into his pocket. He pulled out a granola bar. "Huh. That is not a pen. That's a granola bar that may or may not have spent some time in the ocean."

The bell rang.

"I'll see you later?" Mack asked Brady.

"Maybe during break?" Brady suggested.

"I can't. Study group," Mack replied.

"Lunch?" Brady asked.

"Ah, another study group."

"After school?" Brady tried.

"Oceanography Club dance subcommittee meeting," Mack told him.

Brady was starting to feel annoyed. "How's Easter for you?"

"We've got Marine Biology, right? Third period? I'll see you then," Mack promised, and then she and Alyssa hurried off.

"Mack seems supercool, bro," Devon commented.

"She is," Brady agreed.

"I mean, she actually went right to class when the bell rang. Which is . . . different. And she's wearing socks. But to each their own."

When third period came around, Brady and

Devon got to marine biology class and took seats in the back row. Brady sketched in a notebook while Devon stared, transfixed, into a fish tank.

"How's it floatin', my pucker-faced little buddy?" Devon asked the fish.

Then Brady heard Mack's voice. "Hey!"

He quickly shut the notebook as Mack and Alyssa walked in.

"What are you working on?" Mack asked.

Brady shrugged. "Nothing."

Mack frowned. Was Brady hiding something?

Then a tall, supercute boy walked into the class.

"Mack!" he called out, waving.

Alyssa walked up to him. "Oh, hi, Spencer. Hi," she said awkwardly. "You look great. Like, really, really great. Super great. Perfect, even."

"Thanks, Alyssa, I appreciate that," Spencer said, flashing a sincere smile. Then he turned to Mack. "I was hoping you'd be in this class. I heard you've started an oceanography club. I'm chairing the Environmental Studies Society."

"Really? I wanted to talk to you guys. I thought we could work together on shoreline watershed issues," Mack said excitedly.

Spencer nodded. "Yes! Maybe with an emphasis on habitat restoration and marine pollution."

"I love pollution!" Mack blurted out. "I mean, I don't actually love pollution. But it's an important issue."

"I'm also the head of a club," Brady interjected. "The . . . Surf and Sand Club. Which primarily focuses on surfing. And sitting on the sand. I'm currently the only member."

Mack introduced them. "Spencer, this is Brady."

"I've seen you shred some waves," Spencer told Brady. "You're amazing. It's great to meet you."

He reached out for a handshake, and Brady reached out for a fist bump.

"It's, uh, good to meet you, too," Brady said.

The awkward moment was interrupted by Devon, who introduced himself to Spencer.

"We had PE together. We played that game with the ball and the mesh thing."

"Tennis?" Spencer guessed.

"Yeah, that," Devon replied. "You were much better than me!"

"All right!" Mack interrupted. "Who's ready to dive into some tide pool microbiology?"

The bell rang, and the teacher started class. When it came time for lab work, Brady partnered with Devon, Mack partnered with Alyssa, and Spencer somehow ended up at the lab table with the two girls. Mack, Alyssa, and Spencer worked together smoothly and expertly.

"Centrifuge? Check. Methylene blue dye, check. Cultured petri dish, check," Alyssa checked off as they set up their gear. "Begin inoculation. Let's dilute the solvents!"

Brady and Mack, on the other hand, struggled with their equipment.

"All right, so, here's a blue tubey thing," Devon said. "And a squeezy bulb. And some wet stuff."

Brady was distracted. He couldn't help noticing how close together Mack and Spencer were and how they kept talking to each other. He strained to listen to their conversation.

"Wow, you really know what you're doing," Spencer said, impressed, as he watched Mack combine the liquids in the petri dish.

"You think so? Thanks," Mack said. "I've always loved biology. And the ocean. I should have been born with gills."

"Have you thought about college?" Spencer asked.

Mack nodded. "Of course. I'm knee-deep in applications."

"No, I mean, have you thought about doing *this* in college," Spencer clarified. "There's this new oceanography program at Oregon Coastal College. You spend half the year on a ship, at sea. They'll be at the college fair tonight."

"I'm actually on the College Fair Planning Committee," Mack told him.

"Perfect! I'll introduce you to the college rep," Spencer offered.

Mack smiled gratefully. "That'd be amazing."

Brady stared at them, not sure how he felt about what he was seeing.

"Brady? *Hola?* You okay, my man?" Devon asked.

"I'm good. Totally good," Brady answered. But looking down, he saw that he had gotten his hand stuck inside a beaker. He tried to shake it off.

Crash! The beaker shattered on the desk. Everyone turned to look at him. Mack rushed over.

"Do you guys need any help?" she asked.

"Yes! Totally!" Devon pleaded.

"No, we're good," Brady said.

"I just rocked this experiment," Mack said. "You need to add iodine, agitate, then check out the compound under the microscope."

"I was totally about to do that," Brady said, embarrassed. "Agitate it. Or at least get it slightly annoyed."

Mack nodded and headed back to Spencer and Alyssa. Brady watched her.

Brady. It's us. We're gonna be fine, Mack had told him.

But it was only the first day of school, and Brady wasn't so sure.

Chapter 3

When the last bell of the day rang, Brady eagerly looked for Mack in the school courtyard. She smiled when she saw him.

"Hi! Before I forget, here," she said, pulling a blue rubber bracelet from her backpack. "I'm selling these to raise money for the beach cleanup." The bracelets had SAVE THE BEACH written on them.

Brady nodded. "I dig it."

"Good, 'cause I got you like eight," Mack said, barely fitting one over her own wrist and offering the rest of the bracelets to Brady.

"I'm gonna need a bigger wrist," Brady joked. "Listen, there's a huge swell on. Should we go catch some waves?"

"That sounds awesome," Mack replied. "But I can't. The Save the Beach dance is this weekend. We're up against the wall."

"Speaking of, I had a cool idea," Brady said. "What if you had a dance with a *Wet Side Story* theme? Like, you could do it at the beach. People could wear costumes."

Mack frowned. "That would be totally cool, but we already booked the gym and bought all the decorations. Besides, I think you and I are like the only two people under fifty who've even heard of that movie."

"Yeah, you're right," Brady admitted. "You're sure we can't sneak in a few little awesome waves together before the meeting?"

"Definitely this weekend, after the dance,"

Mack promised. "And anyway, we're going together to the college fair tonight, right?"

Brady made a face.

"Brady, this is important for us. It's our future," Mack told him.

"Yeah. Of course. I'll be there," Brady said, relenting.

"In shoes?" Mack teased.

Brady grinned. "For sure."

Since Mack didn't want to surf, Brady headed home. He and his mom lived in a colorful house on the beach, and Brady had a shack in the back all to himself. Inside he had his own workbench and tools. Many different-shaped surfboards were stacked against the walls.

Brady opened his laptop and pulled up a college application. It asked all these questions about stuff he didn't know the answers to yet. He abandoned it, grabbed a board-planing tool, and went to work on a large surfboard. His mom, Luanne, walked in and watched him for a moment.

"The mad scientist, tinkering away in his hide-out," she teased. "How's the latest board shaping up?"

"Same as all the others," Brady replied. "Slowly. Very slowly."

Luanne nodded and then noticed the application on Brady's screen. "Wow, how's that going?"

"It's going," Brady said. "Opened it up. Stared at it . . ." His voice trailed off.

"They're due pretty soon, aren't they?" Luanne asked.

Brady put down his tool. "It's just . . . everyone seems so focused. They've got their whole lives mapped out. Like Mack. She knows where she wants to go, what she wants to do. And I don't even know what I want for dinner." He sighed.

Luanne read between the lines. "Things were a little rough with you two back at school today?"

"No. Yes. I don't know," Brady replied.

His mom patted his shoulder. "Every great love story hits some bumps in the road, kiddo. Sometimes, the trick is just to keep driving."

"So, love is like a car?" Brady asked.

His mom smiled. "I'm sure you guys will work it out," she said. She turned to leave, and then stopped. "Cereal."

"Huh?" Brady asked.

"That's what you want for dinner. Cereal. It's what you always want," his mom reminded him.

When his mom left, Brady turned on the TV. He restarted *Wet Side Story*, which was always in his DVD player. But this time, with Brady too busy to notice as he worked on a surfboard, the movie played out differently.

Tanner and Lela stood on the beach with Lela's brother, Butchy, and the other surfers and bikers.

"So, Tanner, is youse and me ready to goes and disarm the diabolical weather machine now?" Butchy asked.

"You bet, daddy-o," Tanner replied. "Ready is my middle name."

Seacat, a surfer with a mop of curly hair, looked confused. "I thought Lewis was your middle name," he told Tanner.

"It is Lewis," Tanner said, and then he thought. "It's also Ready. Because that's what I was born. Ready."

"Ready! Right from the moment he was born!" added energetic surfer Rascal.

"Tanner! Don't go!" Lela pleaded. "It's so dangerous!"

"Don't worry, Danger is also my middle name," Tanner replied. "Along with Ready. And Lewis."

"That's a very long name," Butchy remarked.

Lela sighed. "Okay, Tanner. I'll just wait here, and—" She stopped. That was what she was *supposed* to say. But it wasn't how she felt. Not after meeting Mack. "Actually, why don't I come, too? I mean, all we girls do when you guys go off is stand there and do nothing. Maybe I can help."

Tanner looked surprised. "But girls aren't supposed to do that, are they?"

"You're right," Lela said, shaking off that weird feeling she'd had. "I don't know where that came from. Forget it."

Tanner and the boys ran off.

"Go, Tanner! Be safe! You're my hero!" she called after him.

Lela watched them go and then walked back down the beach. Behind her, a blue glow lit up the surf. Then something washed up on the sand. . . .

Mack's lost necklace!

Chapter 4

Brady was still working on the surfboard when he glanced at the clock—and realized he was late to meet Mack! With a start, he jumped up. He grabbed the only clean shirt he could find—a Hawaiian one. Then he grabbed two socks (one blue, one yellow) and reluctantly slipped on some sneakers.

Outside the high school, Mack looked at her watch and sighed. The fair had already started, but there was no sign of Brady.

"Mack?"

Spencer stepped up behind her, dressed sharply in khaki pants and a button-down shirt.

"What are you doing out here?" he asked. "The fair's almost over."

"I'm waiting for someone," Mack explained.

"Well, the Oregon program's about to start packing up," Spencer told her.

Mack looked around, frustrated. She didn't want to miss out. "Then I'd better check them out," she said, and headed inside with Spencer.

When Brady finally arrived, he saw Mack and Spencer walking out of the school, talking to the rep from Oregon Coastal College. He kept his distance and watched them.

"For me, the hands-on approach to ocean-ography just seems amazing," Mack was saying. "Thanks for taking the time to talk to me."

The college rep nodded. "A pleasure. It was great meeting you, Mack. I hope you apply." He shook Mack's hand and walked off.

As Brady listened, it hit him: Oregon. That

wasn't too far, but it was far enough. He had already almost lost Mack to prep school. He couldn't stand to lose her to Oregon.

Brady walked up to Mack and Spencer.

"Hi, Brady!" Spencer said cheerfully.

Brady looked at Mack. "What are you doing here with him?"

"I almost missed the whole fair, waiting for you," Mack shot back. "Where were you?"

Brady shifted uncomfortably. He had never told Mack about his shack or the stuff he did there. She would probably think he was just wasting his time tinkering away at making surf-boards.

"I was, ah . . ." he stammered. "You could have at least sent me a text!"

"I did! Like twelve!" Mack was almost yelling now.

"No, you didn't," Brady insisted.

"Check your phone!"

Brady reached into his pocket. "Uh, I seem to

not have my phone, because I . . . left it . . . somewhere."

"Why don't I just give you guys a second to chat?" Spencer said, backing away.

Mack shook her head at Brady. "Is it too much to ask you to take this one thing seriously?"

"Hey, at least I take *us* seriously," Brady protested.

Mack was stunned. "What? I take *us* seriously! I just spent forty-five minutes waiting outside for you!"

Brady glanced at Spencer. "You weren't exactly waiting alone."

"What? You think . . . Spencer?" Mack lost it. "You were forty-five minutes late! What were you even doing? Did you forget?"

Brady hesitated. Should he tell her?

"I was . . . nothing," he said, looking away.

"You won't even tell me why you stood me up? We used to tell each other everything! What's happening with us?" Mack said.

"I don't know. You tell me," Brady said. "It's like the *school* you doesn't want anything to do with me!"

"This coming from the school *you* that keeps secrets and flakes out on me?" Mack asked in disbelief.

"Well, then, maybe we just don't work at school," Brady said. It hurt to say the words out loud.

"Maybe we don't!" Mack shouted.

"Awesome! So I guess I'll just see you next summer—which is apparently the next time you're free!" Brady couldn't help getting in that last jab.

"Fine by me!" Mack said.

They stared at each other, hurt. Each was waiting for the other to apologize. To take it back. But neither did.

Mack turned and walked away, and Brady watched her go.

Chapter 5

Mack headed for the lagoon and walked onto the pier, staring sadly at the water. Brady had retreated to his shack. He played a sad song on his guitar.

"*It almost feels like it was a dream, all these memories of you and me, blown away in the summer breeze,*" he sang.

In the background, *Wet Side Story* played on the TV in a continuous loop. Brady was too engrossed in his guitar to pay attention to the movie.

The movie was back at the beginning, when

Tanner and Lela first locked eyes. Lela stood on the stage at Big Mama's, singing.

"I just can't stop myself from falling for ya. Can't hold on any longer and now I'm falling for ya. . . ."

She tripped over the microphone cord and fell off the stage. Tanner caught her in his arms.

"Nice of you to drop in," Tanner said, flashing his blinding white smile.

"I guess I literally fell for you, huh? I'm Lela," she began, but then she stopped. "I'm sorry. I can't do this. Put me down."

The music abruptly ended. Everyone turned to look at Lela, confused. This wasn't how the movie was supposed to go.

"Lela, what are you doing?" Tanner asked.

"I don't know. This whole thing, it's just not working for me anymore," Lela admitted. "It's not you, Tanner. You're a great guy—"

"Yes, I am," Tanner agreed.

"But I've got to go!"

Lela hurried out the door, and Tanner raced

after her. She stopped at the edge of the ocean. The night breeze swept her dark hair off her shoulders.

"Lela! What's going on? It's very windy out here. It's not good for my hair," Tanner complained.

Lela turned to look at him. "Ever since Mack and Brady came, I've felt . . . different. Mack wasn't like any girl I ever knew. She inspired me. I miss her."

"I miss her, too. And Brady," Tanner said. "They were swell! But—"

"I want to be like her, Tanner. Try new things, experience new experiences—Wait. What's that?"

Lela spotted something washing up in the waves. Something glowing. She reached down and picked it up. Her blue eyes flashed.

"Tanner! Look at this! Do you know what this is?" she asked.

"Uh, a necklace?" he guessed.

"I gave it to Mack! It's come back to me. Here. Now. Don't you see? It's a sign!"

Tanner was confused. "It really looks like a necklace."

"This means"—Lela turned to look across the ocean—"she's out there. Somewhere. I need to be where she is."

The rest of the bikers and surfers caught up to them. Lela waved.

"Good-bye, Tanner. Good-bye, bikers. Good-bye, surfers. Good-bye, people always standing around whose names I don't know," she called out.

The ocean waves were starting to churn up fiercely. Lela turned to the ocean, and as her necklace glowed brightly, she ran right into the surf.

"We've gotta stop her, right?" Tanner asked, nervously watching her go.

"Sure. I mean, I would," Butchy said. "But water makes me a little nervous."

Tanner started to panic. "What should I do?

Sing a song? That usually fixes everything. Or maybe I should talk in my low voice." Girls loved his low voice. He gave it a try. "Lela! Come back!"

Cheechee, a biker chick with sky-high hair, sidled up to him. "Yeahs, I'd save your low voice for somebody who can actually hears it. She's already in the ocean."

Lela was about to disappear into the waves. A surge of courage rose in Tanner. He bravely bolted in after her.

The dark waves swirled around them. Everything went black for a moment. And then . . .

. . . they emerged from the water onto a sunny beach.

Lela was surprised to see Tanner. "Tanner? What are you doing here?"

Tanner was more surprised by the sun shining overhead. "I don't know. Why is it daytime?"

They looked around. Every hair on their heads was still dry and perfect, just like in the movie. But they weren't in the movie anymore.

Jet Skis zipped across the water as Lela and Tanner walked up the beach, dazed and disoriented.

"What happened? Where are we?" Lela wondered.

Lela saw a para-skier's bright parachute in the air, pulled by a boat.

"That guy's flying!" she cried, amazed. Then she noticed a Jet Ski. "And is that a motorcycle or a boat?"

"I think it's both. He could be in *two* gangs," Tanner guessed. "He could rumble with himself!"

Lela pointed to a restaurant on the beach. "Is that Big Mama's?"

Tanner read the sign. "No, it's Billy's Beach Burgers and Sushi. What's a sushi?" He looked at Lela. "Where are we?"

A teenage boy with spiky hair walked by. Lela stopped him.

"Excuse me," Lela said. "I think we're lost."

"Oh, here. Just use my phone," the boy said.

Cell phones, of course, didn't exist in 1962, when *Wet Side Story* was made. Lela and Tanner stared at the screen, confused. Then the phone spoke to them.

"What can I help you with?" asked a smooth female voice.

"Oh, my! That little box just spoke to us!" Lela said. "Tanner, are we here? Did we make it? Are we in Mack's world?"

Tanner was still focused on the phone. "Hello, lady in the little box. What's your name? I'm Tanner."

Lela turned to the teenager. "We come to your world in peace," she said, speaking slowly and clearly.

Tanner accidentally pressed the button for the forward-facing camera. The phone snapped his picture, and his face appeared on the screen.

"Whoa! How'd I get in there?" he wondered. Then he grinned. "Hi, small me! Lookin' good!"

Chapter 6

Not far away from where Lela and Tanner were, Brady headed across the sand with his board, unaware that his friends were nearby. Brady was just getting ready for his early-morning surf after a night of tossing and turning. He noticed the ocean was flat with an occasional big wave, which wasn't the best condition for surfing. He also noticed a girl picking up trash with a pointy stick. Then he realized that it was Mack!

They locked eyes.

"I thought we weren't supposed to see each other until summer," Mack said.

"I'm just surfing," Brady replied.

"And I'm just cleaning up the beach," Mack said.

Brady smiled smugly. "Really? You're cleaning up at my favorite surf spot?"

"Your surf spot happens to be where there's a lot of trash," Mack said.

Brady was insulted. "What's *that* supposed to mean?"

"It means, there's a lot of actual trash here and I'm cleaning it up," Mack replied. Then her eyes got wide, and she froze.

"Uh, Mack? You okay?" Brady asked.

"Brady, would you think I was crazy if I told you two people who look exactly like Lela and Tanner were walking toward us on the beach?" Mack asked.

Confused, Brady turned around. He saw the boy and girl walking toward them.

"Those people don't look like Lela and Tanner. They *are* Lela and Tanner," he said with awe in his voice.

Mack ran toward them. "Lela? Tanner?"

"Brady! Mack! We found you!" Tanner called out.

Mack reached Lela and crushed her in a hug.

"It's so good to see you!" Lela cried.

"You too," Mack said, smiling at her friend.

"You're really here? In three dimensions?" Brady asked.

Tanner nodded. "I know. It must seem too good to be true. But it is!"

"I missed you," Lela said, squeezing Mack again.

"I missed you, too!" Mack said. "I think about you all the time."

Brady tapped her shoulder. "Ah, Mack. Can I just take a quick second to highlight the little fact that *they.* Are *here*?"

"Wow! Yes!" Mack exclaimed. She looked at Lela. "Why? How?"

"I found the necklace," Lela said, showing it to her.

Mack was confused. "But I lost it in the ocean."

"It floated back to me," Lela explained, tucking it absentmindedly back under her shirt. "I knew it was a sign! I had to find you. So I carried the necklace into the waves, questioning my whole existence—"

"I never question anything," Tanner interrupted. "I just followed her."

"And the next thing we knew, we were here!" Lela finished.

"Ah, one quick question," Tanner said. "Where, exactly, is 'here'?"

"We're on the beach, silly!" Lela said.

"Oh, right," Tanner agreed. "But, like, what country are we in?"

Mack and Brady exchanged looks. They had never explained to Lela and Tanner that they weren't real, only characters in a movie.

"Let's just call it the future," Brady replied.

"The future?" Tanner screwed up his face, thinking hard. "Like, it's already tomorrow, today?"

"Maybe a few days *after* tomorrow," Brady said.

Tanner grinned. "Cool!"

"Cool! It's way cooler than cool!" Lela exclaimed.

From out of nowhere, music swelled, just like it would have in a movie before the characters broke into song.

Mack looked at Brady. "So they magically brought music with them?"

"In a word, yes," Brady replied.

They watched, helpless, as Tanner and Lela sang a song about how cool it was to be in the future.

"I think I'm gonna love it here, because it seems like the kind of place where I can follow my dreams," Lela sang.

"This is right where I wanna be," Tanner sang with her. As Tanner and Lela sang with all their hearts, other kids on the beach watched in amusement.

When the song was finally over, Lela announced, "I don't think I'm ever going to leave here! Come on, Tanner. Let's take a walk on this crazy beach of the future!"

She grabbed his hand and pulled him away to frolic in the water, leaving Brady and Mack in an awkward situation. They were still in a big fight—but now they had a problem they needed to solve together: figuring out what to do. Nobody else would understand.

"What are we going to do with them?" Mack asked Brady. "I mean, they're from 1962. They could get into serious trouble."

"Come on. Lela? Tanner? What kind of trouble could they get into?" Brady asked.

They heard laughter, and turned to see Tanner and Lela fascinated by the automatic sensors in the beach showers, laughing and making a big scene. A small crowd had gathered to watch the strange kids in old-fashioned clothes.

Brady sighed. "Yeah. What *are* we going to do with them?"

Then Mack noticed something as the shower water splashed over Lela and Tanner.

"Their hair. It's dry," she said.

"Just like when they surf in the movie," Brady added.

Mack frowned. "Brady, they don't belong here. Remember what happened to us when we were in their world? We almost got zapped out of existence. I don't know what's going to happen to them if they stay in ours, but it won't be good. We've gotta get them home. We should just tell them the truth. They're made-up characters in a 1962 beach movie."

"Wouldn't that kind of totally blow their minds?" Brady asked.

Mack sighed. "You're right. They couldn't

handle it," she admitted. "So maybe we just show them that our world isn't as great as they think it is. So they *want* to go back."

Now it was Brady's turn to look thoughtful. "Then . . . they'd just have to carry the necklace right back into the ocean and beam themselves home."

Mack nodded. "Exactly. But it's not going to be easy. So in the meantime, we should probably keep their identities secret. So the whole world doesn't freak out."

Brady glanced at Lela. She was staring in fascination at a remote-control helicopter.

"Amazing! How did they find a pilot so small?" Lela asked herself.

Brady shook his head. "Good luck with that. We'll need a cover story. Exchange students or cousins or something."

"Good call. I'll take Lela, you take Tanner. We'll meet up at school," Mack said. "I'm still mad at you."

"Yeah, well, I'm still mad at you, too," Brady said. But neither of them sounded entirely convinced.

They looked at each other shyly for a minute and then headed off to round up Lela and Tanner.

Mack brought Lela back to her house.

"So, if you're going to come to school with me, you need to look . . . less like you look," Mack said, taking in Lela's sixties hairdo and old-fashioned (but supercute) dress.

Mack pulled a plain blue dress out of her walk-in closet. "This is good. Not too flashy."

Lela took it and headed into the closet to change. When she came out, she was wearing the blue dress—but now it looked like it was from the sixties! The skirt flared out, and there was a big belt around the waist. Lela even had a matching blue bow in her hair.

More movie magic, Mack thought. There had to be some way around it. She handed Lela a plain T-shirt and jeans.

Lela went into the closet and came out again—still looking like a sixties movie character. The jeans had become capris, the T-shirt sported little capped sleeves, and now a red patent leather belt circled her waist.

"Great," Mack said under her breath. "First singing, now this!"

Brady wasn't sweating things as much. His mom worked nights, so it wasn't an issue to have Tanner sleep over. They ran into her as they left the house the next morning.

"Oh, hello," Luanne greeted them, surprised.

"Mom, this is . . . Dolf," Brady lied. "He's an exchange student. From Iceland. I volunteered for him to stay with us for a few days."

Tanner shot him a confused look, then nodded and played along. He knew that Brady must have some reason to not reveal his true identity.

Luanne raised an eyebrow. "Well, that's a surprise."

"Yeah, sorry, it was kind of a last-minute thing," Brady said.

His mom smiled. "Okay. Iceland. Wonderful." She turned to Tanner. "Our house is your house. It's great to meet you."

"That's how everyone feels," Tanner replied brightly.

Brady groaned inwardly.

Bringing Tanner to school wasn't going to be as easy as he'd thought.

Back in the movie, the bikers and surfers were feeling pretty uneasy without Lela and Tanner around.

"I'm feeling a little lost here, peoples," Butchy announced. "Ever since Lela and Tanner walked off into the ocean, I got the sense that things should be happenin' that ain't happenin'."

"We could rumble," suggested a biker named Lugnut. "That always cheers you up."

"I does love a rumble, but no," Butchy said.

"It feels like that ain't supposed to happen right now."

Then he had an idea. "Maybe somebody should sing something, like Lela might have done if she was heres. Cheechee, sing something!"

"But I was doing my nails!" Cheechee complained. Reluctantly, she took her chewing gum out of her mouth, placed it behind her ear, and started singing "Falling for Ya," Lela's song.

Butchy watched, worried. It still didn't feel right.

"Seacat, maybe youse should get up there and help her out," he suggested.

"Sure," Seacat said, jumping up to sing Tanner's part. But the song sounded totally different when Cheechee and Seacat sang it. And when it came time for Cheechee to fall off the stage . . .

Thud! She landed on the floor. Seacat didn't catch her.

BRADY BLINDFOLDED MACK AND TOOK HER TO THE EXACT
SPOT WHERE THEY HAD MET THREE MONTHS EARLIER.

MACK WAS BUMMED OUT WHEN SHE REALIZED THE NECKLACE
LELA HAD GIVEN HER HAD FALLEN INTO THE WATER.

BRADY AND HIS BEST FRIEND, DEVON, WERE WAY BETTER
SURFERS THAN SCIENTISTS!

BRADY WAS TOO EMBARRASSED TO TELL MACK HE DESIGNED AND
BUILT SURFBOARDS. SHE DIDN'T EVEN KNOW ABOUT HIS WORKSHOP.

MACK FELT TERRIBLE THAT "SCHOOL BRADY" WASN'T SIMPATICO WITH "SCHOOL MACK."

AFTER LELA FOUND THE NECKLACE, SHE DECIDED SHE NEEDED TO BE WHERE MACK WAS.

TANNER WAS IN LOVE WITH THE SMARTPHONE'S CAMERA.
"HI, SMALL ME! LOOKING GOOD," HE SAID AS HE GAZED AT HIMSELF.

MACK AND BRADY COULDN'T BELIEVE LELA AND TANNER
WERE ON THEIR BEACH!

LELA LOVED EVERYTHING ABOUT SCHOOL. "I NEVER KNEW LEARNING COULD BE SO MUCH FUN!" SHE EXCLAIMED.

THE *WET SIDE STORY* CREW FREAKED OUT AFTER ONE OF THEIR FRIENDS DISAPPEARED INTO THIN AIR.

MACK TOLD LELA AND TANNER THEY WERE JUST
CHARACTERS FROM A MOVIE.

TANNER AND LELA REMOVED THE EMBLEM FROM THE OLD
SURFBOARD SO THEY COULD PUT IT ON THE HYDRO-LITHIUM BOARD
BRADY HAD BUILT AND GET BACK TO WHERE THEY HAD COME FROM.

MACK TOLD BRADY SHE'D BUY HIM A MANGO SMOOTHIE
IF HE DIDN'T LIKE THE MOVIE.

ALYSSA AND SPENCER HELPED MACK SELL TONS OF TICKETS.

LELA, QUEEN OF THE BEACH WAS A HUGE HIT
AT THE SCHOOL DANCE.

Shaky, Cheechee got to her feet. "I think some of my hair may have broke."

Butchy shook his head. "This don't feel right. None of it."

Behind him, one of the surfers sparkled magically—and then vanished. . . .

Chapter 7

The next morning, Lela and Tanner followed behind Mack and Brady as they walked up to the high school.

"This is perfect. School," Brady whispered to Mack. "It'll make them hate our world. Nobody likes school."

"Hey, I like school," Mack protested.

"Yeah, but you're weird," Brady teased. "Take Lela to Calculus with you. Ten minutes of heavy math and she'll be begging to go home. I'll try to keep Tanner out of trouble."

Mack nodded, then turned to Tanner and Lela.

"Okay, we've got some ground rules for you," she said.

"Don't do anything that gives you away," said Brady.

"No hair wetting," said Mack.

"No clothes changing," added Brady.

"And Tanner, don't do that thing with your teeth," Mack told him.

"This thing?" Tanner asked, smiling.

Ping! His teeth gleamed.

"Yeah, don't do that," said Brady.

"And most of all . . ." Mack began.

"No singing!" she and Brady said together.

"Just one song?" Lela asked.

"No!" Mack and Brady said firmly.

Then Mack and Lela headed to class, and Brady and Tanner took off down a different hallway.

"Okay, stay close to me," Brady told Tanner as they walked through the crowded halls of the high school. "Just walk down the hallway and be cool."

"You got it!" Tanner replied. "There's one thing I can do better than anyone, and that's walk down a school hallway."

He snapped up his collar and began to strut down the hall, greeting everyone he passed.

"Hey, how's it going, big daddy? Looking good," he told one guy. Then a girl walked past. "Hi, name's Tanner. Hang ten, cookie."

Tanner started getting weird stares. Then Devon showed up.

"Brady! Greetings, meister-bro," he said, doing the surfer handshake with his friend. Then he noticed Tanner. "Who's this dude?"

"This is, uh, my cousin Dolf," Brady replied. "From Iceland."

Tanner shrugged and smiled.

"Dolf! What's up?" Devon asked.

"The ceiling?" Tanner guessed.

Then he noticed Devon's spiked-up hair.

"Your hair is very pointy!" Tanner remarked.

"Thanks, bro," Devon replied. "It's amazing what you can do with a screwdriver and some surf wax."

Tanner pointed to the perfect wave of hair on his head. "I use my own secret mix of coconut juice and rubber cement," he confessed.

"Rubber cement! Wicked! What a great idea!" Devon turned to Brady. "I love this dude! Later, dawgs."

Brady breathed a sigh of relief as Devon walked off and pushed Tanner toward their first class.

A short while later, Mack ushered Lela out of Calculus. She had hoped that Lela would hate it enough to want to go back to her own world.

"So, what'd you think of Calculus?" Mack asked. "Pretty brutal, right? That's what life is like in the modern world. Lots of tough classes."

"I loved it!" Lela crowed, her blue eyes shining. "It's magical! The integral accurately gives the area under a formula while the derivative predicts its instantaneous slope at any point!"

Mack looked surprised. "Wow, you really got it, didn't you?"

Lela smiled. "Who knew thinking could be so fun?"

Spencer approached them. "Mack! Hey, who's this?"

"This is my cousin. Ah, Delga. From Finland," Mack replied.

Lela trusted Mack knew what she was doing. She nodded agreeably.

"I see the resemblance," Spencer said, smiling at Lela. Then he turned to Mack. "Listen, I hope I didn't cause any problems with you and Brady last night."

Mack shook her head. "No, our problems are totally our own."

"Fair enough," Spencer said. "Hey, how's the big dance shaping up?"

"Okay. We haven't sold many tickets," Mack replied.

"I'm sure people will come. It's a good cause," Spencer said. "Maybe you can save me a dance. Purely as friends, of course."

"Ah . . . maybe?" Mack said. She still hadn't sorted out her feelings about Brady. Spencer seemed to like her, but it was too much all at once.

"Great. I'll catch you later, then," Spencer promised.

"There's a dance tonight?" Lela asked as Spencer walked off. "How fun! This world just gets better and better."

"Yeah, until your formerly adorable boyfriend starts acting like a completely different person," Mack said with a sigh. "You're better off in your world, Lela, where boys are simple. And more reliable."

Alyssa walked up to them. She raised an eyebrow when she saw Lela.

"Who's the girl in the crazy dress?" she asked.

"Lela. Hi," Lela said, confidently thrusting out her hand. "I'm here to discover who I am and find fulfillment."

Alyssa looked at Mack, impressed. "A woman who knows what she wants. I like her!" She turned to Lela. "I did my philosophy camp thesis on female self-empowerment."

"I can rebuild a motorcycle," Lela offered.

"Really? I'm thinking of buying a scooter," Alyssa said, and she and Lela walked off together, talking excitedly.

She's never going to want to leave, Mack thought. *But then what will happen to her?* Mack shuddered just thinking about it.

"It's a disaster. She loves everything," Mack reported to Brady later, as they waited in the cafeteria's lunch line.

"I think I might be wearing down Tanner a little," Brady said.

Ahead of them, Tanner held up something. "Nuggets made out of chicken! Amazing!"

"Or not," Brady said. "Don't worry. I've got a plan. It's gonna for sure break their spirits. We need to turn them loose, alone, in the most dangerous, frightening, confusing place imaginable. A place where one false move results in mockery, exile, shame, and horror." He gestured with his right hand. "The high school cafeteria."

Brady and Mack approached Tanner and Lela.

"All right, you guys are on your own," Brady told them. "Find a place to sit. Make friends. Good luck!" Then he and Mack ran off.

Tanner and Lela got their lunch and carried their trays to the tables in the quad outside. Tanner nodded at a table of football players.

"Hi! I'm new here," he said cheerfully.

"I could care less, spray tan," one of the guys said.

Tanner didn't lose his smile. "Actually, the name's Tan-ner. No 'spray.'"

The football player stood up. "Get out of my face!" he growled.

Tanner and Lela backed up. They realized everyone was staring at them.

"Tanner, are you getting the feeling that everyone here is kind of standoffish and meanish?" Lela asked.

"Right. And angryish, too," Tanner replied. "Like the surfers and bikers. Only angryish-er."

Brady and Mack watched the scene from across the quad. It looked like their plan was working.

And then they heard the music.

"Oh, no," Mack groaned.

Tanner and Lela started to sing a song about how they wanted everyone to be friends. But that wasn't the worst of it. Everyone stood up and joined in the song. The whole school was dancing and singing! And movie magic was making them do it!

Mack and Brady joined the other students as they danced around the cafeteria. Cheerleaders danced with nerds. Jocks danced with kids from the band. Then the music ended, and everyone sat down where they were. Nobody was sure what had just happened.

But the weird thing was nobody was mad. The song had worked. Everyone was in a better mood. Tanner and Lela happily waved to the crowd.

Mack sighed. "Our plan is definitely *not* working!"

Chapter 8

After a long, strange day, the final school bell rang. Tanner walked outside with Devon and Brady. Devon was listening to music on his earbuds.

"Dude, you got some bodacious pipes!" Devon told Tanner, talking loudly over the music only he could hear. "You totally have to join my surf band. I play a gnarlicious didgeridoo."

"Thanks! Why are we talking so loudly?" Tanner shouted back.

Devon didn't hear him. "Later, my hombre!" he said with a wave.

Then Tanner saw Lela with Alyssa and Mack and walked over.

"Lela! Hi! You wanna hang out?" he asked her. "I've been working on some new looks. I call this one 'Thoughtful Handsome.'"

He made the face for her, resting his chin in his hands.

"That's wonderful, Tanner, but I can't," Lela replied. "I'm sorry. Mack and I are going to do some calculus homework together. It's so exciting!"

Tanner was confused. "Okay, well, have fun. Without me."

Mack pulled Brady aside. "We're further than ever from talking them into going back."

"Just stay with Lela," Brady told her. "Keep working on her. I'll take Tanner."

Mack nodded, and they went their separate ways. Brady took Tanner to his shack and handed him his tablet.

"Here, play with this," he said. "Try to hit those pigs with the little birds."

"Ooh, neat," Tanner said, taking it from him. But he played only a few seconds before he put it down.

"Brady, can I level with you?" Tanner asked.

Brady nodded. "Sure."

"I don't usually like thinking about things," Tanner explained. "But I've been thinking about something. I've always assumed that Lela would always be there for me. But that night when she ran into the water with her necklace, it gave me a strange feeling in my stomach. It felt like when I drink a milk shake too fast. Like maybe things wouldn't work out."

"That's called worry," Brady told him.

"Yes! That," Tanner said. "And the thing is, things *always* work out for me. But here—I'm worried that Lela wanted to come to this strange world because I wasn't enough for her."

Brady had never seen Tanner look so sad. But he knew how his friend felt.

"I know what you mean," Brady said. "Like,

you're with a girl, and suddenly she's got her whole life figured out, and you just feel a little left behind."

Then he realized something. "I guess all you can do is be the best dude you can be, and hope that's enough," he added.

"Is that what you do with Mack?" Tanner asked.

Brady shook his head. "No. Recently, we've kind of hit a rough patch. I've been spending a lot of time working on something I haven't told her about."

He walked to his workbench and pulled off a blue tarp, revealing the strange-looking surfboards he'd been working on.

Tanner's eyes got wide. "Are those surfboards?"

"Yes," Brady said. "These are all boards. Boards that do what other boards don't. Like this round one. It has rotating fins, so you can surf in any direction."

"You made these? Neat! I've never made anything." Tanner said. He pointed to a huge board on Brady's workbench. "What's this one?"

"This one's crazy," said Brady. "It's got these two intake manifolds here, leading to sealed hydro-turbines hooked up to an internal lithium-ion battery."

"Everything you just said? I have no idea what that means," Tanner admitted cheerfully.

"Basically, this is a surfboard that moves by itself," Brady explained. "If it works. I haven't tested it."

"Why can't you tell Mack?" Tanner asked.

"Because I'm not sure if she'd get me spending so much time on something like this," Brady replied. "She's got her life mapped out."

And I don't, Brady thought. *Not yet, anyway.*

Tanner nodded. "I understand, Brady," he said. "Maybe the problem is you're not tan enough!"

❧

While Brady and Tanner talked in the shack, Mack and Lela talked in Mack's bedroom.

"I love everything here!" Lela was saying as she looked through all the modern items on Mack's dresser. "The challenging classes. The interesting conversations. The flavored lip gloss! Vanilla kiwi-berry? It's delicious *and* keeps my lips moist!"

Lela moved to Mack's closet next and started trying on clothes.

"Lela, our world isn't all that great," Mack said. "There's finals, and taxes, and global warming. You really had it good back in your world. Your hair's always perfect. You have a boy who loves you."

"*You* have a boy who loves you, too," Lela pointed out. "But you want more, right? You want to live your life to the fullest. I want more, too."

Mack paused. Lela had a point. But she couldn't admit that. She had to convince Lela to go back.

"No," Mack said. "Being with the right

person can actually make life more full. If you both have the same drive, the same passions. Unless he doesn't respect your passions . . . and keeps secrets from you . . . or gets weird when you're busy."

Mack flopped down on the bed. "I don't know! It's all pretty confusing here—which is why you should go home."

Lela stepped out of the closet, wearing an outfit of Mack's. She looked great—and perfectly present-day. The magic necklace glittered around her neck.

She's becoming part of this world, Mack thought. *That's what happened to me and Brady before we almost disappeared forever!*

Mack ran into the hallway and quickly called Brady.

"We have a situation," she told him. "Meet me on the beach—and bring Tanner!"

The four friends met up a few minutes later. Tanner grinned when he saw Lela.

"Wow, Lela! You look like . . . future Lela. Groovy!" he said.

"Very groovy!" Brady added.

"No, not groovy at all," Mack said. "She's not supposed to look modern. Tanner, smile."

Tanner obeyed—but there was no *ping!* this time.

Then she pulled Tanner over to the beach showers and turned them on, dousing him with water.

"Hey!" he cried. His perfect hair was soaked.

"Look! It's wet!" Mack cried.

"What's happening?" Tanner asked, panicked, as he felt his wet hair. "My hair feels so squishy! And limp! I don't like this feeling!"

Mack pulled Brady aside. "Don't you see? The very essence of who they are is changing. They could get stuck here forever! Or the whole fabric of our reality could split open! We've gotta get them back."

Brady thought. "Let's just tell them the truth,"

he said. "About who they are and where they really came from."

"But weren't we worried about what it might do to them?" Mack asked.

"We're running out of other options," Brady said.

Mack nodded. She turned to Tanner and Lela and took a deep breath.

"Tanner, Lela—you're just made-up characters in a movie. You're not real," she said.

Brady winced. "Okay, maybe I would have eased into that a little more gently."

"What? A movie? I don't understand," Lela said, her voice shaking. She fidgeted with the necklace.

Mack opened her phone and found an image of the movie poster for *Wet Side Story*. She showed it to Lela and Tanner.

"Hey, it's us!" Tanner said. "Doing things we usually do."

"See, you guys get to live inside this awesome

imaginary world," Brady explained. "A movie world. My favorite movie. It's how Mack and I met."

Lela's blue eyes were full of fear. "But I don't want to live in a movie world."

"But you do," Mack said. "That's why your life was so perfect, Lela." She turned to Brady. "How can we make them understand?"

Brady smiled. "We could try explaining it in their language," he said, and music swelled behind him.

"Do we have to? Really?" Mack asked, and then she sighed. "Fine."

Then Brady and Mack started to sing, trying to convince Tanner and Lela that life was better in the movies.

"You gotta play the scene, up on the silver screen. No matter where you've been, good times are moving in!" they sang together.

"No!" Lela yelled, abruptly ending the song. "I'm sorry, but I don't want to be that girl anymore. I don't want people to write my lines for me. I want to stay here. Forever."

Then she tore off the necklace and threw it into the ocean with all her might.

Chapter 9

Back in the movie, Butchy and the gang were hanging on the beach at night when Cheechee ran up with Giggles, a blond surfer girl.

"Oh, my gosh . . . you're not . . . gonna believe this," Cheechee said, out of breath. "We was walking with our pals Muffler and Sidecar. And then *boom!* They just up and vanished."

"This is terribles!" Butchy cried. "Peoples are vanishing left and rights! Any of us's could be next!"

He got thoughtful. "Things started going

wrong ever since Lela and Tanner took off."

"You think thems leaving is somehow coronated with this chain of events?" Cheechee asked.

Butchy nodded. "Yeahs. I do," he said, and then he spotted something in the sand. "Hey, what's that?"

He jogged over and picked up Lela's necklace, which had washed up onto the shore. He grabbed it.

"My sis used this when she disappeared into the ocean," he said, remembering. "Maybe wese can use it, too. We can find Tanner and Lela and bring them back and make everything normal again."

"We're leaving?" Cheechee wailed. "Then I need to go home and get some hairspray!"

"There ain't no time, Cheechee!" Butchy said. "We gotta get there now! Before more peoples starts disappearing."

He took a deep breath. He was afraid of water, but he was even more afraid of disappearing forever. He raced into the waves, and the bikers and surfers followed him.

The sun was setting on the beach, but Mack was not giving up her search for Lela's necklace.

"It's gone, Mack," Brady said.

"It might still wash up," Mack said, continuing to search.

"Last time, it ended up in a parallel movie universe!" Brady pointed out.

"Do you have any better ideas? Just keep looking," Mack snapped.

"Don't take this out on me," said Brady. "I wasn't the one who just blurted out, 'Hey! Lela! Guess what? You're not real!' "

Mack put her hands on her hips. "Really? This is my fault? How was I supposed to say it?"

Brady shrugged. "I don't know. You could've been a little less . . . direct."

" 'Less direct'? Like, we should have kept it a secret?" Mack asked. "That's been working well for you lately."

Tanner and Lela watched them argue.

"Why are they fighting? They're not in rival gangs," Tanner said.

"Here I guess couples do it, too," Lela said.

"Guys!"

A familiar voice rang out across the beach. Lela looked up to see her brother, Butchy, stumble out of the waves! And there was Seacat, and Cheechee, and Struts, and Giggles, and Lugnut! And other kids from back home.

Mack and Brady heard the commotion.

"Are you kidding me?" Mack asked.

Brady's eyes got wide. "The whole *cast* is here?"

Butchy hugged Lela. "We did it! We found youse guys!"

"Uh, nice to see you guys," Brady said. "What are you doing here?"

"What do ya mean, what are wese doing here?" Butchy asked. "We's here to take Lela and Tanner home."

"Yes!" Tanner cried.

"No," Lela said flatly. "Butchy, I don't want to go home."

Butchy looked perplexed. "But, Lela, I'm your brother. Don't you miss me? Don't you miss all of us?"

"Yes, of course, a lot!" his sister replied. "But I'm starting to find myself here, Butchy. I'm happy."

"Okay, that all wells and goods and all. But here's the thing, see: peoples back home have been disappearing," Butchy told her.

"Peoples?" Lela asked.

Butchy nodded. "Yeah. They just sparkle. And then—*poof!*—they vanish."

"And we don't even knows wheres to! Or if they's coming back!" Cheechee added.

Mack turned to Brady. "That's what's happening. Lela and Tanner are the stars of the movie. Without stars, there's—"

"No movie," Brady finished. "It's vanishing out of existence."

"You guys have to go back," Mack told Lela and Tanner. "Otherwise all of you will disappear."

Lela's eyes looked sad. "I understand. I have to go back. It's our job. To be characters in a movie."

She turned to Mack. "I'm going to miss you," she said.

"Me too, Lela," said Mack. "But I'm so glad I got to see you again. And somehow, I know we'll always be friends. Even when we're in different worlds."

They hugged. Tanner shook Brady's hand.

"Good-bye, Brady," Tanner said.

"Good-bye, Tanner," Brady replied. "Take care of yourself. It was so great to see you again. Now, you guys get yourselves home."

The *Wet Side Story* kids headed back into the ocean. Mack and Brady looked at each other. Without Lela and Tanner there, things were awkward between them again.

"Well, that's done," Brady said.

"I should get to the dance," Mack said. "It's time to start setting up."

"I guess I'll just see you there," Brady said, and they both walked off in different directions.

Out in the water, Butchy held the glowing necklace.

"We should be zapped back any second," Lela said.

Something was bugging Tanner. He looked back over his shoulder and saw Mack and Brady walking in two different directions.

"Wait!" he said. "I'm worried about Mack and Brady. They're not happy. We can't just leave them like this. That's not what friends do, right? We can't go home until we get them together."

"Tanner, I've never seen you like this," Lela said. "You're caring about someone besides yourself. I like it."

Tanner smiled.

"Wait, what about the disappearing and

stuff?" Butchy asked nervously. "Do we have time? What'll happen?"

"I don't know," Tanner replied. "But I know it's the right thing to do."

Chapter 10

The Save the Beach dance in the high school gym wasn't exactly the most exciting dance ever. A deejay spun tunes while a handful of kids stood under the blue crepe paper party decorations. A few of them even danced.

Brady was standing by himself when Devon approached him.

"You all right, dude?" he asked.

"Sure. I'm good," Brady replied in a voice that definitely did *not* sound good.

Across the gym, Mack halfheartedly untangled some balloon strings. Spencer walked up.

"Great party."

"The turnout's a little low," Mack said. She fidgeted with the blue SAVE THE BEACH bracelet she had on. "I guess the school gym wasn't the most exciting venue."

"Maybe it'll pick up," Spencer said. Then he paused. "Hey, I have a question for you."

Time to nip this one in the bud, Mack thought.

"Spencer, please don't take this the wrong way. You're a good-looking guy. But I'm just not . . . looking for anything right now," she told him.

"You think that I like you?" Spencer asked. He sounded confused.

"Ah, yeah. Don't you?" Mack asked.

"Oh, no. Sorry," Spencer said. "You're a wonderful person. But I like Alyssa."

Mack gazed at her friend. Alyssa was dancing like some kind of puppet whose strings were being pulled by a monkey.

"Alyssa?" Mack asked.

Spencer nodded. "Yeah, we hung out at

this government conference this summer. She was . . . wow . . . She blew my mind."

"But Alyssa made me think that you thought *I* was cute," Mack said.

Spencer looked sheepish. "Yeah. Sorry. Thing is, I haven't had the best luck with girls. My buddies said the best way to impress a girl is to make her jealous. So I told Alyssa I liked you."

Mack shook her head. "That's terrible advice," she said.

"Yeah. Now that I actually say it out loud, it does sound completely stupid," Spencer admitted.

Mack gave him a little push. "Just go! Be nice to her! Dance with her!"

Spencer headed out and started dancing along with Alyssa. Mack and Brady stayed on opposite sides of the gym, not even looking at each other.

Then the gym doors burst open and some of the *Wet Side Story* kids poured in. Mack and Brady looked stunned.

"Oh, no," said Mack.

The roar of an engine filled the gym as Butchy rode in on a motorcycle. Tanner rolled in behind him on a Segway and made a beeline for Brady.

"What are you guys still doing here?" Brady asked.

"I'm here for you, Brady," Tanner replied.

Brady was surprised. "For me?"

"We couldn't leave, Brady. We realized we had some unfinished business," Tanner explained.

"Are you crazy? The movie is vanishing! You're all in danger!" Brady couldn't believe they hadn't left.

"It's not right that things aren't right between you and Mack. So we're here to help you make them right!" Tanner added.

Lela looked at Tanner with a new respect. "Isn't it great, seeing Tanner like this? So concerned and thoughtful? I'm so proud of him."

Tanner and Lela smiled at each other adoringly, then he turned to Brady.

"Brady, when we were doing that worry thing

about Lela and Mack, I think you forgot about something really important. See, we have a word in our world. It's called 'confidence,' spelled K-O-N . . . fidence."

"We have that word, too, Tanner," Brady said.

"Well, you need to remember it. You're a good surfer, and a good friend, and you make cool things. You're an amazing guy! And I'm pretty sure the only person who's keeping you from realizing it is, well, you."

Brady nodded slowly. "I can't believe these words are about to leave my mouth, but . . . Tanner, you've just said the smartest thing I've heard all day."

He spotted Mack across the dance floor. "I've got this," he said confidently, and the magical movie music started up behind him.

"I gotta be me," he started to sing, and soon everyone in the gym was singing and dancing along. Brady grabbed Mack and the two of them danced and sang together.

Brady jumped up onstage to sing the final verse of the song. Then, just like Lela had in *Wet Side Story*, Brady tripped over the microphone cord and fell off the stage!

Mack caught him in her arms.

"I guess I literally fell for you, huh?" Brady said, quoting from the movie.

Then the two of them collapsed in a heap, giggling.

Suddenly, Butchy appeared, holding up the necklace. "Okays, everyones," he announced, "I hate to interrupt this bee-yutaful moment, but we's gotta get back to whatever's on the other sides of that scary watery stuff."

"He means the ocean," Cheechee translated.

"Yeah, that," Butchy said.

"Butchy's right," Tanner said. "We've gotta get going before another one of us—"

Suddenly, Butchy started to sparkle. Then he disappeared—holding the necklace!

"—vanishes," finished Tanner, stunned.

"Butchy!" Lela screamed.

The other kids at the dance didn't notice—except for Devon.

"Whoa! Did you guys see that?" he asked Alyssa and Spencer, but they were slow-dancing and gazing into each other's eyes.

Devon looked into the cup he was holding. "I gotta lay off the punch."

Brady stared at the spot where Butchy had just been. "He's gone."

"With the necklace," Mack added.

Lela's eyes were wet with tears. "My brother . . ."

Mack put a hand on her shoulder. "Lela, I'm sorry."

"This is really happening!" Lela cried. "We're losing ourselves. What are we going to do? How can we get home? How can we make all this right again? Before we all vanish?"

Nobody replied. Then Lela answered her own question.

"Wait. When you guys first came to our world,

you didn't have the necklace, because I hadn't given it to you yet," she said, remembering. "How'd you get there then?"

"Lela, you're a genius!" Mack cried.

She and Brady hurried to her house on Brady's bike. The magic surfboard that had taken them to Lela and Tanner's world hung on the wall in her bedroom. The yellow surfboard had a medallion embedded in the surface. Shaped like a flower, the medallion glowed faintly—just like the necklace!

They brought the board to the beach. Stars glittered in the black sky. Most of the other movie kids had vanished already. Only Tanner, Lela, Seacat, Lugnut, Giggles, Struts, and Cheechee were left.

"Finally!" Cheechee cried.

"Everyone's disappearing," said Struts.

"Just like Butchy!" Giggles added.

Then . . . *poof!* Struts and Giggles vanished!

"We've gotta hurry!" Lela cried.

Brady held out the magic surfboard. "This will take you home."

"Are you sure?" Tanner asked.

Poof! Seacat vanished.

"Yeah," Brady said, shaken. "I sure hope so. Just paddle out and catch a big wave."

Then he froze. "Oh, no."

He stared out at the completely calm ocean.

"There's no surf," Mack said.

"But how can we surf if there's no surf?" asked Lela.

"You can't," Mack said, defeated.

Cheechee looked down at herself. She was sparkling.

"Oh, no," she said. "Good luck, guys!"

Poof! Cheechee vanished.

"Tanner! It's just us!" Lela wailed.

"We have to get back. Now," Tanner said firmly. "Before our movie is gone forever and we vanish, too!"

Chapter 11

"But how? You need waves to surf, don't you?" Lela asked.

Brady looked at the magic surfboard. Suddenly, he had an idea. He ran to his bike and grabbed a small toolkit.

"Tanner, remember how you said you've never made anything?" Brady asked.

Tanner nodded. "Yeah?"

"I need your help making something," Brady said, handing Tanner the toolkit. "Take my bike kit. Use it to try and pry the emblem off the board."

"Hey, I can help, too," Lela offered. "I'm good with tools."

"Awesome," Brady said. He turned to Mack. "In the meantime, we need to swing to my place."

Brady led Mack back to his house. Then he walked past it, toward his secret shack.

"Where are we going? We passed your house," Mack said.

"We're not going to my house," Brady said. He stopped in front of his shack.

Mack raised her eyebrows. "Oh."

"Come on up," he said, climbing the stairs.

Mack followed him. "What is this place?" she asked, looking around.

"It's kinda my personal workshop-slash-chill-out space," Brady explained.

Mack noticed all the surfboards around the room. A look of awe dawned on her face.

"Wait. What're all these?" she asked.

"Surfboards," Brady replied. "Kind of. Some of them are just prototypes."

"You made them? From scratch?" Mack asked.

Brady nodded. "It's not as hard as it looks," he replied. "Well, it's about exactly as hard as it looks."

Mack suddenly got it. "This was your secret."

"Yeah," said Brady. "I've been making boards. But not just any boards. Boards that do cool new things."

He pointed to one nearby. "This one's like a catamaran, so it really flies."

"Why couldn't you tell me?" Mack asked.

Brady sighed. "Because, well, you're so together. College, your whole oceanography thing. You've got a vision for your life, your future. And here I am, just making boards. I wasn't sure you'd, I don't know . . . respect it."

Mack's eyes widened. "Brady, this is incredible!" she exclaimed. "My grandpa spent his life making boards. It's an art. And what you're doing, this is the next level. This *is* a vision for your life. An amazing one."

"You really think so?" Brady asked.

Mack nodded. "I do."

"Good!" He pulled the tarp off the big board he'd been working on. "I've been making this one for us."

Mack ran her hands along the almost-finished board. The longboard was beautifully crafted. It had an odd shape, and Mack could see a large lump toward the back, down by the fins.

"The only bummer about our summer was those days when there was no swell, when we couldn't surf together. So I had this idea," Brady explained as he quickly worked to add the finishing touches to the board. "What if we didn't need a swell? This board has a motor built in."

"So you can surf, even when there's no surf," Mack said.

"Any day we want. No matter what," added Brady.

"It's beautiful," Mack said softly.

Brady struggled to get the hatch covering the motor closed, but it finally shut.

"If this baby actually works, with the magic emblem on it, it might just take Tanner and Lela home," he said hopefully.

"I know I should have told you about it sooner," Brady admitted. "I'm sorry."

"Brady. I'm sorry," Mack said. "I'm sorry you ever felt like you had to hide this from me. Do you want to know the only thing that really matters to me about our future?"

"What?" Brady asked.

Mack smiled. "That we're in it together."

They gazed into each other's eyes. Finally, they understood each other. All the bad feelings that had been around since school had started washed away.

"It's ready," Brady said. "Now or never."

As they left the shack, Mack noticed the poster of *Wet Side Story* on the wall. Characters and words were disappearing, one by one. Worried, she hurried back to the beach with Brady.

Tanner and Lela ran up to meet them.

"We got the pretty flower off!" Tanner said. Then he noticed the new board. "Hey, that's the manifold . . . hydro . . . lithium . . . board. The one that can surf by itself."

"Exactly," Brady said. "There's some tire glue in the kit. It should do the trick."

Lela handed him the glue, and Brady quickly cemented the emblem to the board.

"Let's get it down to the water," he said, and Tanner and Lela grabbed the board and waded into the ocean.

Mack hung back.

"You okay?" Tanner asked.

Mack nodded toward the nearby mangrove trees. "Do you know where we are?"

Brady looked around. "The clearing in Dolphin's Cove."

"Where we met," Mack added. "Brady, if this

doesn't work, and Lela and Tanner vanish and the whole movie never even existed, doesn't that mean that we never would have met? If they don't make it . . . we won't even know each other."

Brady hugged her and managed to smile. "How could you ever forget me?"

Mack smiled back. There was nothing to do now but hope. The two of them joined Lela and Tanner at the water's edge.

"I guess this really is good-bye, this time," Mack said.

Brady hugged Tanner. "Thanks for everything, man. Honestly, I'm glad you came," he said. He looked at Mack. "We needed it."

"You're welcome, Brady," Tanner replied.

Mack hugged Lela. "I'm so glad I got to see you again."

"Me too, Mack," Lela said. "I'll never forget you. Again."

"Me neither," Mack said, and then she looked

into Lela's eyes. "Listen, Lela. When you go back to your world, it doesn't have to be the way it was. Start a math club. Invent a new flavor of lip gloss. Change the movie. Make it *your* story."

Lela smiled. "Thanks, Mack. I will."

Then Mack took off her blue SAVE THE BEACH bracelet. She had decorated it for the dance with a version of the magic flower. She put it on Lela's wrist.

"I'll treasure it forever, Mack," Lela promised.

They hugged one last time, and Tanner and Lela carried the board into the ocean. Brady jogged into the water to coach them.

"Okay, try to stand," Brady instructed them. "Find your balance."

Lela and Tanner stood up on the board.

"Good," said Brady. "Tanner, hold on to this T-bar. Lela, hold on to Tanner. Bend your knees, keep your weight forward. Steady yourselves. Once this thing goes, it's going to go fast."

Brady put his hand on the start button.

He took a deep breath and pushed it.

Nothing happened.

"What's wrong?" Lela asked.

"I don't know," Brady replied. He pushed it again, and nothing happened. He tried a third time, and the motor still wouldn't start.

Suddenly, Lela and Tanner started to sparkle.

"Oh, no! It's happening!" Tanner cried.

"There must be something wrong with the propulsion system!" Brady exclaimed. "Hang on!"

He dove under the water and opened the hatch. There was a problem, all right.

He emerged from the water. "I can't fix it without a screwdriver."

Lela pulled a bobby pin out of her hair. "Will this work?"

Brady grinned and dove back under. He quickly worked to make the repair. When he surfaced again, Lela and Tanner were sparkling like crazy.

"This is our last chance! Get ready!" Brady yelled. "Come on!"

He pushed the button, and the motor roared to life. The surfboard blasted off, carrying a sparkling Lela and Tanner out to sea.

Then they vanished into two streaks of light.

Chapter 12

Brady tumbled out of the swirling water. He ran back up the beach, toward Mack . . . and then right past her, without even looking at her.

That was because they hadn't met yet.

Instead, Brady ran up to Devon, who was waiting for him. They launched into their surfer handshake.

"Bro-heim! I told you! Night bodysurfing! Mondo spiritual, right?" Devon asked.

"It was totally flat, dude," Brady replied, shivering. "Let's get out of here. I'm freezing."

As they walked off, they noticed Mack, standing alone.

"Who's that?" Brady asked.

"No idea, bro," Devon replied. "I think she might go to our school. She's in the ocean club or something."

"She's kinda cute," Brady said.

Mack didn't notice the two surfer boys. As she stared at the waves, a tingling sensation traveled up her spine.

That's weird, she thought. It was like she was supposed to remember something, but she couldn't.

Mack shrugged off the feeling and walked back up to Billy's Beach Burgers and Sushi. The Save the Beach dance was in full swing. Mack was elated; the dance was more successful than she had hoped. They'd been able to rent a giant movie screen to set up in the parking lot. Everyone had loved the idea of airing a sixties teen beach movie on the beach. They even got into wearing costumes from the film!

As Brady and Devon biked past the restaurant, the music caught Brady's attention.

"Whoa. What's going on there?" he wondered.

"I think it's that dance thing," Devon replied. "There were fliers at school."

"They're going to project a movie?" Brady asked. "It looks kind of awesome. You wanna check it out?"

"When have you ever known me to pass up a possible fiesta?" asked Devon.

They headed to the party. Alyssa and Spencer were selling tickets at the door.

"Mack! Where have you been? Sales are through the roof!" Alyssa reported when Mack showed up. "You're a genius. People love the theme!"

Brady and Devon walked up.

"Can I help you guys?" Mack asked.

"Yeah," Brady replied. "I gotta ask. What's with the screen? And the costumes?"

"It's a fund-raiser," Mack explained. "We're saving the beach. It's a 1962 drive-in movie party."

"Cool. How'd you come up with that idea?" Brady asked.

"I don't know. It was just inspired, somehow." Mack smiled at him.

"What movie are you showing?" Devon asked.

Mack nodded to a poster on the wall. It showed the kids from the *Wet Side Story* movie. Except the title was changed. Now it was called *Lela, Queen of the Beach*. And Lela was leading the pack.

A shiver traveled up Brady's spine.

That's weird, Brady thought. It was like he was supposed to remember something but couldn't.

"*Lela, Queen of the Beach*?" he said.

"You've never heard of it?" Mack asked.

"Oh, I've heard of it. Everyone has," Brady answered.

"Good!" said Mack. "Then we agree it's pretty much the most awesomest movie ever made."

"I don't think 'awesomest' is a real word,"

Brady said. "And even if it was, I'm not sure that movie's exactly my jam."

"This *film* was totally ahead of its time," Mack told him. "It's a visionary take on female empowerment and self-expression. It's the reason I love to surf."

"You surf?" Brady asked.

"Of course," Mack replied. "How about this: come inside, check it out. If you don't totally dig it, I'll buy you a mango smoothie."

Brady grinned. "I do love mangos."

"Sounds like you win either way," Mack said.

She put a blue SAVE THE BEACH bracelet on his wrist. There was a moment of familiarity.

She led him to the party. "Wait here," she told him.

She climbed onstage, and the music stopped. All eyes turned to Mack as she spoke into the microphone.

"Thank you all for coming!" she began. "We

totally blew away our expectations and raised a ton of money for the beach. And now, the moment you've all been waiting for . . . *Lela, Queen of the Beach!*"

Everybody cheered wildly, and the movie started to play on the screen. It looked a lot like *Wet Side Story*, except Lela was front and center this time. The bikers and surfers started to sing, and the kids watching the movie started to dance along.

"Really?" Brady asked.

"Come on," Mack said, grabbing his hand. "Sometimes you've just got to spontaneously burst out into song."

Brady relented and joined in the singing and dancing. Mack led the dance-along in sync with the kids on-screen.

Lela looked down from the screen at Mack and Brady dancing. Mack felt eyes on her and looked up to see Lela, who seemed to be staring right at her! Lela held out her hand. Was that a SAVE THE

BEACH bracelet around her wrist? Lela gave her a wink and a smile.

Mack got that weird feeling again. Then Brady smiled at her, and looked into her eyes. As they began to slow dance, a whole new feeling took over. A feeling that everything was happening exactly like it was supposed to.

"I'm Mack," she said.

"I'm Brady."

And somewhere, on a beach far away, a necklace washed up onto the sand . . . and started to glow.